MODERN ROLE MODELS

Shaun White

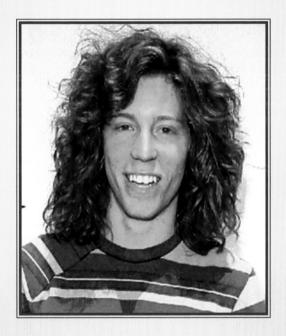

Karen Schweitzer

Mason Crest Publishers

Produced by OTTN Publishing in association with
21st Century Publishing and Communications, Inc.

MASON CREST PUBLISHERS INC.
370 Reed Road
Broomall, Pennsylvania 19008
(866) MCP-BOOK (toll free)
www.masoncrest.com

Printed in the United States of America.

First Printing

9 8 7 6 5 4 3 2

Library of Congress Cataloging-in-Publication Data

Schweitzer, Karen.
   Shaun White / Karen Schweitzer.
      p. cm. — (Modern role models)
   Includes bibliographical references.
   ISBN-13: 978-1-4222-0493-1 (hardcover) — ISBN-13: 978-1-4222-0780-2 (pbk.)
   ISBN-10: 1-4222-0493-6 (hardcover)
    1. White, Shaun, 1986–   —Juvenile literature. 2. Snowboarders—United
States—Biography—Juvenile literature. I. Title.
GV857.S57W557 2009
796.939092—dc22
[B]   2008020416

Publisher's note:
All quotations in this book come from original sources, and contain the spelling and grammatical inconsistencies of the original text.

CROSS-CURRENTS

In the ebb and flow of the currents of life we are each influenced by many people, places, and events that we directly experience or have learned about. Throughout the chapters of this book you will come across CROSS-CURRENTS reference boxes. These boxes direct you to a CROSS-CURRENTS section in the back of the book that contains fascinating and informative sidebars and related pictures. Go on. ▸▸

CONTENTS

American snowboarder Shaun White can't seem to believe that he has just won a gold medal in the 2006 Winter Olympic Games. "I'm a little overwhelmed right now. I can't explain it," the 19-year-old admitted to reporters as he celebrated his victory in the men's halfpipe event with family and friends.

The Quest for Gold

SHAUN WHITE HAS ESTABLISHED HIMSELF AS one of the greatest **action sports** stars in history by claiming nearly all of snowboarding's highest honors and dominating **vert competitions** in professional skateboarding. He was the youngest person to ever win the U.S. Open Snowboarding Championship and the first athlete to win a **gold medal** in both the Summer and Winter X Games.

In addition to being one of the most accomplished action sports stars, Shaun is also one of the highest paid. He earns money from competitions, his own product lines, by appearing in movies, and by **endorsing** products for various companies. He has been

CROSS-CURRENTS

If you'd like to learn more about the early days of Shaun's sport, check out "History of Snowboarding." Go to page 46. ▶▶

a household name for years and a full-fledged celebrity since the 2006 Olympics.

⇒ MAKING THE TEAM ⇐

To qualify for the 2006 Olympic team, Shaun needed to perform well in the Chevy Grand Prix series, the most important competition in the snowboarding world. Altogether, 105 talented boarders would compete on the **halfpipe** during the five-event series, hoping to land one of 16 positions on the U.S. team. Each rider would be judged on his two best finishes. The top scorers would win places on the team.

CROSS-CURRENTS

"Making the U.S. Winter Olympic Snowboarding Team" provides information about what is required to compete in the Olympics. Go to page 47. ▶▶

The first event was held in December 2005. Shaun won the top spot, beating out the closest competitor by two-tenths of a point. He took first place again at the second qualifying event.

Although his two straight victories virtually guaranteed Shaun a place on the Olympic team, he didn't stop there. Shaun went on to win the third, fourth, and fifth events in the series. It was the first time a rider had won every halfpipe contest of the season in the history of the Grand Prix.

⇒ HIGH EXPECTATIONS ⇐

Because of Shaun's unique ability to land several major tricks during the same run down the halfpipe, everyone expected him to win the gold medal in that event during the Winter Olympics in Turin, Italy. Before the games began, U.S. halfpipe coach Bud Keene remarked on Shaun's talent:

> **"Going into a 1080 [three full rotations in the air] with a 900 [two-and-a-half rotations]—no one else has been able to do that. Shaun is head and shoulders above the rest. He's clearly the guy to beat [in Turin]."**

Unfortunately for Shaun, winning wasn't as easy for him as everyone thought it would be. When the halfpipe competition began, he fell on his first qualifying run and didn't automatically make it into the finals. Shaun admitted later the pressure got to him:

Shaun impresses the Olympic crowd with a high-flying move during a halfpipe run. Shaun's score of 46.8 in the first round of the finals was the best of the competition, and earned him the gold medal. His spectacular tricks made him an audience favorite, and by the time the Olympics ended Shaun was among the most popular American competitors.

> **"I'm just dropping in, and it hit me: I'm at the Olympics. I wasn't even looking at the halfpipe. I was looking at the crowd, going, 'Wow.'"**

After his fall, Shaun knew he would have to step up his performance during the next qualifying run if he wanted to continue. He had a quick talk with the U.S. coach and climbed back up the pipe to try again. His second run was much better. He landed every trick he tried and easily made it to the afternoon finals.

⇒ EARNING A SPOT ON THE PODIUM ⇐

Riders get two runs in the finals of the Olympic halfpipe competition, but only their best score counts. Shaun's first run started out perfect. He soared more than 25 feet into the air on his first jump and then landed one of his favorite tricks, the **McTwist**. He followed up with consecutive 1080s and back-to-back 900s.

The five judges gave Shaun a score of 46.8, the best of the day. Shaun watched as 10 other riders tried to beat his score. The only competitor who came close was U.S. teammate Danny Kass, whose best score was 44.0.

At the 2006 Winter Olympics Shaun (center) outrode 10 other snowboarders in the finals of the men's halfpipe competition. They included his countryman Danny Kass (right), who won the silver medal, and Markku Koski of Finland (left), who finished third. The American medalists are pictured here waving to the crowd at a ceremony in Turin, Italy.

When the last rider, Markku Koski, fell, Shaun knew he had the gold. He celebrated the moment by throwing his hands into the air, hugging his coach, and then meeting his teary-eyed family at the bottom of the hill. Afterwards, he told reporters:

> **❝I didn't know if I would win gold. I just knew I wanted it. This is the best year of my life. I'm so happy my whole family's here. I know I won't have this again. It's amazing, everybody's having such a good time.❞**

Winning an Olympic gold medal was an amazing accomplishment for Shaun. Only 84 of the 2,500 athletes who competed in the 2006 Winter Games won gold. Reflecting on things afterwards, Shaun said the reality of his victory did not actually sink in until the next day:

> **❝I woke up and saw my medal next to my bed, and I'm like, 'Wow this really went down.' I met my family for breakfast. They were like, 'No matter what you do, you're always going to be known as Shaun White, Olympic gold medalist.'❞**

⇛ OLYMPIC GOLD MEDALIST ⇚

Shaun's popularity had been growing for years, but he became a real celebrity after winning the gold at the Olympic Games. Fans were desperate to meet him and many people in the media wanted to interview him. After his win, Shaun appeared on *The Today Show*, *Late Night with Conan O'Brien*, *The Tonight Show with Jay Leno*, and a slew of other talk shows.

The sudden rush of fame might have been hard for some people to deal with, but not Shaun. A couple of months after the Olympics, he commented that he was enjoying his newly earned celebrity status, saying:

> **❝I think it's fun. I've waited my whole career to get to that point where I can sit back and say, 'What do I really want to do now?' And everybody's supporting it. That's the coolest thing, to have opportunities.❞**

From an early age, Shaun enjoyed skiing and snowboarding with his family. In this photo, Shaun (right) is pictured with his older sister, Kerri, at one of Shaun's early snowboarding contests. Although he was often the youngest person riding in amateur events, Shaun's talent enabled him to regularly beat his much older opponents.

Growing Up on the Slopes

SHAUN ROGER WHITE WAS BORN ON SEPTEMBER 3, 1986, to Kathy and Roger White of Carlsbad, California. He grew up in this suburb of San Diego with his sister, Kerri, and brother, Jesse. Shaun took to the slopes at a young age. When he was only four years old, he was skiing on June Mountain with his family.

Unfortunately, life wasn't all fun and games for the future Olympian. At a young age, Shaun was diagnosed with a heart condition known as tetralogy of Fallot. Doctors had to perform two separate surgeries to fix his damaged heart. This slowed Shaun down for a little while, but not for long.

Like any other little brother, Shaun wanted to do everything his older brother Jesse did. When Jesse started skateboarding at the YMCA and in the backyard, Shaun skated too. And when Jesse showed an interest in snowboarding,

CROSS-CURRENTS

Tetralogy of Fallot is a rare heart condition. To learn more about this childhood disease, see "What Is Tetralogy of Fallot." Go to page 48. ▶▶

Shaun wanted to learn, also. To this day, Shaun says it was Jesse who inspired him to try tricks:

> **"He taught me all the grabs and spins and stuff like that. He told me to do stuff and I'd go try it and maybe land it."**

⇶ Too Young for Lessons ⇷

Finding somewhere for Shaun to take snowboarding lessons wasn't easy. Although the White family took frequent trips to ski resorts like Bear Mountain, Mammoth, and Mount Hood, the resorts did not offer snowboarding instruction for kids under the age of twelve.

Shaun's dad solved this problem by taking snowboarding lessons himself, then teaching his children everything he had learned. It wasn't long before Shaun was zooming down hills so fast his mother began to worry. She made him promise to ride **switch**—facing back toward the top of the hill. But riding backwards didn't make Shaun ride slower—it just made him ride better!

Shaun made further progress after enrolling in Windell's Snow-board Camp in Mount Hood, Oregon. Director Tim Windell admitted later that they almost didn't allow Shaun to attend the camp:

> **"We almost didn't take him, because he was only 6 or 7 at the time, and we'd never had such a young camper. But he was an incredible athlete, even at that point in time."**

At the age of seven, Shaun entered and won his first amateur snowboarding contest. The win earned him a wildcard entry for the 12-and-under division of the United States Amateur Snowboard Association (USASA) National Championships. Even though most of the riders were several years older, Shaun finished among the top 15 competitors.

⇶ Amateur Champion ⇷

Shaun was a natural in the snow, but he did have a problem that his family feared might hold him back. His board was too big, because no one made snowboards for children his age.

Snowboarders gather at the bottom of a run at the Mount Hood ski resort in Oregon. Mount Hood was one of the White family's favorite places to vacation when Shaun was growing up. As he grew better at snowboarding, Shaun was permitted to attend a snowboarding camp at the resort to develop new skills.

To find a board that would fit Shaun, his mother called Burton, a snowboard manufacturer. The company found a smaller board for Shaun. Even better, Burton officials were so impressed with Shaun's skill and enthusiasm that they offered to **sponsor** him when he was only seven years old.

The following year, Shaun returned to the USASA competition. This time, he won first place. By the time Shaun was 13 years old, he had won four more national amateur titles and a pile of trophies. It was clear that he could not accomplish much more as an amateur. It was time to go pro.

RISING TO THE CHALLENGE

Dominating the competition on the amateur circuit had been easy for Shaun. Going pro in 1999 presented a whole new set of challenges. The riders were all better, faster, and stronger. Shaun was also much younger than most of the other competitors, and

Ten-year-old Shaun is much smaller than the audience members watching him walk up a hill with his board at the 1996 U.S. Snowboarding Open. But despite his size, Shaun was a fierce competitor who proved to be absolutely fearless on the slopes. After dominating amateur snowboarding competitions, Shaun turned pro when he was just 13 years old.

everyone seemed to notice. He later spoke about how he wanted to earn the respect of his fellow riders:

> **❝I wanted to be recognized more for my riding talent than my age. I wanted to make that step from being the cute little kid to being associated with the older riders.❞**

It didn't take long for Shaun to get his wish. In 2000, he qualified for the X Games and placed 15th in the **superpipe** event. Shaun continued to enter every snowboarding contest he could. Within a year, he was placing in the top ten in major competitions.

⇒ A TRUE PROFESSIONAL ⇐

CROSS-CURRENTS

To learn how the X Games evolved into the world's best-known action sports event, read "History of the X Games." Go to page 49. ▶▶

The year 2001 brought new accomplishments. Shaun entered two events in the Winter X Games, **slopestyle** and superpipe, and placed in the top ten in both contests. He also swept the Vans Triple Crown series and won the Arctic Challenge with the unanimous vote of his fellow competitors.

By the time the 2002 snowboarding season began, Shaun was no longer the pint-sized kid who could get **big air**. He was a seasoned professional, a major player among the best competitors in his sport. At the Winter X Games that year, Shaun won two **silver medals**. He continued to place well in other contests.

⇒ A RARE DISAPPOINTMENT ⇐

After **shredding** with the pros and racking up great scores for two years, Shaun decided to try out for the 2002 U.S. Olympic Team. He was 15 years old at the time. This was only the second Winter Olympics in which snowboarding was included as a sport; the first had been in 1998.

Although Shaun's effort was very good, he ultimately came up 0.3 points short of securing the final spot on the men's team. This was a disappointment, but Shaun didn't let it get him down. He immediately moved on to the next snowboarding competition—as well as getting involved in a whole new sport at the professional level.

Shaun White—instantly recognizable by the shock of red hair flying around his helmet—gets big air while performing a trick at a vert competition. It is rare for an athlete to be able to perform at a high level in more than one sport, but by 2003 Shaun was able to successfully compete in professional skateboarding events.

Two-Sport Superstar

DURING THE SUMMER OF 2002, SHAUN BEGAN TO focus more on skateboarding. He had been skating in his backyard and at the Encinitas YMCA with his brother and their friends since they were very young. Shaun was so talented that the previous year, he had been asked to join the legendary professional skateboarder Tony Hawk on a summer skatepark tour.

Tony, who had been skating with Shaun for years, encouraged him to consider going pro:

> **"** Even five years ago, I thought Shaun was one of the most amazing athletes on the planet. I first saw him snowboarding when he was about nine, and he was just this little pixie with a giant helmet,

CROSS-CURRENTS

For the story of skateboarding legend Tony Hawk, Shaun's friend and supporter, read "Who Is Tony Hawk?" Go to page 50. ▶▶

coming down the halfpipe. Now, he's grown into his own style—plus he can do tricks five feet higher than everyone else does them. **"**

As intriguing as the idea of going pro was to Shaun, he decided it might be best to get through the snowboarding season before making any new commitments. The first snowboarding competition of 2003 was approaching and he wanted to do well.

⇒ TWO BIG WINS FOR SHAUN ⇐

Shaun had won two silver medals at the 2002 Winter X Games. What he really wanted in 2003 was gold. He worked extra hard preparing for the 2003 games, which would be held in Aspen, Colorado, during January. Shaun was slated to compete against other snowboarders in the slopestyle and superpipe events.

When the games began, the first snowboarding event was the superpipe. Shaun's competition included future Olympic teammate Danny Kass and 2002 Olympic gold medalist Ross Powers. Shaun had near-perfect runs his first and second times out. His first run score was 97.67 and his second run score was 97.00. Danny Kass and Markku Koski came very close, but in the end they weren't able to beat his highest score. Shaun won his first X Games gold medal.

The slopestyle contest was held the next day. Shaun rode so well that the other competitors couldn't come close to touching his score. In his winning run, which was scored 95.00, he did a 720° rotation over a 57-foot gap, a tricky grind on a rail, and one of the best 900s ever seen in a snowboarding event.

Winning two gold medals at the Winter X Games was a phenomenal achievement. Only one other competitor had ever won two different events at the games. (Ross Powers had done it in 1998.) After winning the slopestyle event, Shaun told reporters:

"I've always wanted to come to the X Games and do good. So I guess this is my year. . . . I'm stoked. **"**

It certainly was Shaun's year. He was named the Outstanding Athlete of the 2003 Winter X Games. He also won a lot of prize money and a new SUV. Shaun probably would have driven the vehicle home, but he wasn't old enough to drive yet!

This multiple-exposure photograph shows Shaun launching and landing a 900—a trick that involves two-and-a-half aerial turns-during the slopestyle competition at the 2003 Winter X Games in Aspen, Colorado. Shaun overpowered his opponents on the course at Buttermilk Mountain, winning gold medals in both the slopestyle and halfpipe events.

➤ MAKING HISTORY ➤

The U.S. Snowboarding Open was Shaun's next big competition. Everyone was still talking about his performance at the X Games. Most people expected him to do just as well at the U.S. Open.

One of the events Shaun would be competing in was called the Rail Jam. In this brand new U.S. Open event, riders were required to perform tricks on long rails and staircases. Shaun rode really well in the competition and was awarded second place behind fellow rider Travis Rice.

After the Rail Jam, Shaun moved on to the slopestyle event. He took the lead on his first run and never lost it. Shaun rode so well that the other 19 competitors simply couldn't keep up. The win was monumental for Shaun because it made him the youngest person to ever win the U.S. Open slopestyle event.

X GAMES GO GLOBAL

In 2003, ESPN decided to create a Global X Games event. The games would be held in May in San Antonio, Texas, and in Whistler, British Columbia. Competitors from six continents were scheduled to compete in summer and winter sports, including skateboarding, BMX, in-line skating, motocross, skiing, and snowboarding.

Shaun would be representing the U.S. team in the men's super-pipe event. After watching him win the U.S. Open and take home two gold medals at the Winter X Games just a few months before, everyone knew that Shaun was the guy to beat. Nevertheless, his win certainly wasn't guaranteed. Talented snowboarders from all over the world would be competing, and they all wanted to win gold for their team.

The superpipe competition was held in British Columbia. The superpipe was made entirely from snow. At 60 feet wide, 16 feet high and 500 feet long, it was much larger than the average half-pipe. The judges expected the riders to use every inch of the pipe in the competition.

Shaun was in top form on the day of the event. During practice, he navigated the icy pipe easily. When it was time to make his first run, Shaun slid down the superpipe and landed one daredevil trick after another. He was awarded a 97.00—the best score of the day. On his second run, Shaun did even better. His 98.00 score won him the gold medal in the competition and helped the U.S. team earn much needed points.

When the 2003 snowboarding season ended, Shaun was the top-ranked snowboarder in the world. He had won gold medals at all four of the major snowboarding contests that year: the X Games, Vail Sessions, Vans Triple Crown, and the U.S. Snowboarding Open. He also won several minor snowboarding events. Overall, Shaun earned hundreds of thousands of dollars in prize money. Shaun's sponsors, which included the department store chain Target, ski goggle manufacturer Oakley, and snowboard maker Burton, were very pleased. They began to promote Shaun as the newest superstar of action sports.

⋙ ALL EYES ON SHAUN ⋘

Friends had been trying to convince Shaun to become a professional skateboarder for several years. In 2003, he finally decided to give skating a shot. He ended the snowboarding season earlier than normal so that he could get ready for the skating season.

Shaun's first contest as a pro skateboarder was the 2003 Slam City Jam North American Skateboarding Championships. The annual Slam City Jam is the oldest and one of the most respected skateboarding events in North America. Shaun would be skating in the vert contest against experienced competitors like Andy Macdonald, Bucky Lasek, and Pierre-Luc Gagnon.

As always, Shaun wanted to do well. If he could place high enough, he would earn the opportunity to skate in the X Games,

CROSS-CURRENTS

It is rare for an athlete to succeed at several sports. For stories about some who have, see "Other Two-Sport Athletes." Go to page 51. ▶▶

which were scheduled to take place in the summer. Shaun told a reporter a few months later how he felt about entering the Slam City contest:

> ❝It was my first pro contest—so scary, but it was something I had to do to figure out whether I wanted to [be a pro skater] or not.❞

Shaun knew everyone would be watching to see if a snowboarder could keep up with the best skaters in the world. He had three runs to get a good score. Only his best score would count.

On his first run, Shaun earned an 86—a very good score. Shaun fell on his second run and was awarded a 64. On his third and final run, Shaun received an 84.6. Overall, it was a solid performance. Shaun finished fourth, behind Sandro Dias, Andy Macdonald, and Jake Brown. This earned Shaun a spot in the Summer X Games.

⋙ WELCOME TO SUMMER X ⋘

Shaun's participation in the Summer X Games was a very big deal because it was **unprecedented**. No athlete had ever qualified to participate in both the Summer and Winter X Games. The accomplishment made Shaun the center of attention.

During the summer, he partnered with new sponsor Mountain Dew, did a back-to-school commercial for longtime sponsor Target, and appeared in a cartoon on the Nickelodeon network. He was even awarded an ESPN Espy Award for Best Action Sports Athlete.

Shaun also became the face of the Summer X Games. For a while, an 80-foot image of him could be seen on towers along L.A.'s Sunset

Shaun, then 16 years old, stands in front of an enormous advertisement in Los Angeles for the 2003 Summer X Games. That year Shaun made history by becoming the first athlete to compete in both summer and winter sports at the X Games. Although he did not win a medal in the skateboarding event, Shaun did finish a respectable sixth.

Boulevard. The images were advertisements for the Summer X Games and helped to make Shaun even more of a household name.

In between photo shoots, Shaun began investing the prize money he had won. He told *Snow* magazine:

> **"Most of my money just goes into the bank. My mom helps me with investing it, we've bought three houses—one we live in and the other two are rentals. . . . Luckily, most of the decisions [we've made] have been good ones."**

Most of the time, however, Shaun practiced hard for the Summer X Games. He knew that he would be skating against the best competitors from all over the world. Some of the biggest names in skating, like Bucky Lasek, Bob Burnquist, Andy Macdonald, and Rune Glifberg would be there. Shaun needed to be ready.

The 2003 Summer X Games were held in August in Los Angeles, California. Shaun skated very well and took sixth place in the vert event. He didn't win a medal, but he did make history by qualifying and competing.

⇒ STILL A KID ⇐

By the time he turned 17 in September 2003, Shaun White was officially a two-sport superstar. He had traveled the world a few times over. He had won cars, gold medals, and more prize money than most people could imagine. He also had the support of sponsors and a worldwide fan base.

But there was one thing that made Shaun White just like any other kid: he had to study and go to school. This wasn't always easy given his travel schedule. Shaun tried to get as much schoolwork done as he could throughout the winter, but he often found himself stuck inside throughout the summer trying to catch up.

A teacher sometimes traveled with him to help Shaun out. However, Shaun was still required to attend classes at Carlsbad High School. Luckily for him, the school was flexible. He got gym credits for skating at the YMCA, art credits for picking the graphics on his own line of skateboards, and economics credits for handling the heavy financial responsibilities that came with winning so many competitions.

Shaun gets big air off the lip of a halfpipe during a competition. Although Shaun's 2004 season was a disappointment, in 2005 he proved that he was among the world's top snowboarders *and* skateboarders. He won another Winter X Games gold medal, and also earned his first major victory as a professional skater.

Dominating the Competition

SHAUN WAS ON TOP OF HIS GAME AT THE beginning of 2004. He was invited to return to the Honda Session at Vail. This cutting-edge snowboard competition was in its second year and drew a huge crowd. Shaun had won first place in both the rail contest and the slopestyle contest the previous year, so everyone expected a repeat performance.

Not surprisingly, he lived up to everyone's high expectations. He took the top spot in the rail contest one day and the top spot in slopestyle the next. Shaun won $30,000 at the event. However, although Shaun didn't know it at the time, this was one of the few cash prizes he would earn in 2004.

➤ A DEVASTATING INJURY ➤

Shaun was the main attraction when the 2004 Winter X Games opened. He had won two gold medals the previous year and was

25

fresh off his Session at Vail success. Everyone was watching to see if he could continue the streak.

Things were good for Shaun at first. He won the gold medal in the slopestyle contest with a score of 96.00. The win seemed so effortless that most people thought he would do the same in the superpipe contest the next day.

A huge crowd turned out to watch him qualify for the finals. Shaun's first qualifying run went off without a hitch. He posted the best score of the day. But something went wrong during his second run. Shaun felt a sharp pain in his knee. The pain was so bad that there was no way he could continue. He dropped out of the finals and went home with only one gold medal. Afterwards, Shaun told *Sports Illustrated for Kids* how upset he was about getting injured in the middle of the competition:

> **"I had such a great score in the first [halfpipe] qualifying run. And then I felt this weird thing in my knee and I was like 'What is that?' That night, it hurt more when I had to walk up the stairs to get into the condo. It was awful having to walk away from that pipe, probably the best pipe I've ever ridden."**

⇒ TIME OFF ⇐

In the spring of 2004, Shaun had surgery to correct his injured knee. It was tough for him. His muscles shrank from **atrophy** after the procedure. He had to go to rehab and the gym to rebuild his body.

Shaun was so eager to compete again that he started snowboarding before the injury had time to heal completely. He ended up hurting himself even worse and was forced to miss all of the summer skating competitions and most of the fall snowboarding season.

CROSS-CURRENTS

For more details about the action-filled video glimpse into Shaun's life, check out "The Shaun White Album." Go to page 52. ▶▶

⇒ SHAUN ON DVD ⇐

Rest and rehab were not the only things Shaun did in 2004, though. He also released a **documentary** called *The Shaun White Album.* Shaun's sponsor, Mountain Dew, helped him to promote the behind-the-scenes snowboarding movie by giving out free CDs

In 2004, the 17-year-old seemed headed for a great year, but a knee injury during the Winter X Games ended his snowboarding season early. Watching from the sidelines without being able to compete was very frustrating for Shaun. He skipped the entire pro skateboarding season that year so that he could recover fully from his injury.

containing video clips of the movie. Shaun's fans were also able to enter a contest offered by Mountain Dew. First prize was a trip for four to Colorado and a snowboard lesson from Shaun.

When the movie premiered, Shaun invited his family and a few friends, including skateboarders Tony Hawk and Bucky Lasek, to watch with him. Everyone ate candy and enjoyed the flick. Afterwards Shaun admitted in an interview that he was nervous about putting the movie out:

> **❝I was so scared that I was going to put out a bad movie. If I didn't like the movie after I saw it edited, I would have pulled the plug and have had to pay back the sponsors hundreds of thousands of dollars.❞**

As it turned out, DVD sales of *The Shaun White Album* were fairly good, making the project another success for Shaun.

A TRIUMPHANT RETURN

By winter, Shaun felt that his knee was fully healed. He tested it in December 2004 by signing on to participate in the annual Air and Style contest. This is one of the largest European snowboard events. Riders are required to complete two different jumps. Each of the competitors is judged on the difficulty of their tricks, and they are awarded points for style and flair.

Although Shaun had won this competition in 2003, some people wondered if he was physically ready to compete against some of the best snowboarders in the world. Shaun proved himself by landing two near-perfect tricks: a switch frontside 900 and a switch frontside 360. For the second year in a row, he won the contest.

GOING FOR GOLD AGAIN

Shaun was only getting started. He kicked off 2005 with a trip to the Winter X Games, signing up once again for both the slopestyle contest and the superpipe contest. Shaun was hoping for gold in both events.

Everybody was starting to get used to Shaun taking first place in nearly every competition he entered, so it was no surprise when he easily won gold in the slopestyle event. However, the superpipe contest did not go nearly as well. Shaun's performance was solid, and he earned a score that would have won on most days—just not that day. He finished in fourth place, behind Danny Kass, Andy Finch, and Antti Autti.

SKATEBOARDING VICTORIES

Shaun had another important victory in 2005, but this time it wasn't in a snowboarding contest. It was a vert competition on the Dew Tour. Shaun's first-place finish was his first major win as a professional skateboarder.

At the Summer X Games, Shaun competed in the regular vert contest as well as the best trick contest. Shaun won a silver medal in the vert event, and used every one of his runs in the best trick competition trying to land a 1080—a trick involving three full rotations, which nobody had ever been able to do. He made 29

Shaun shows off his trophy from the 2005 Dew Tour Skateboard Vert Championship event held in Louisville, Kentucky. This was Shaun's first win in a major pro skating competition. A few weeks later, Shaun proved that his win was no fluke, finishing second in the vert event at the 2005 Summer X Games.

attempts in all, continuing even after the competition had ended, but he wasn't able to successfully land the trick.

Despite his failure in the best trick competition, people were impressed with Shaun's determination. Shaun's repeated attempts to land the difficult trick made people realize that beating the other competitors was not his ultimate goal. He confirmed this later, telling a reporter:

> **"I put tons of pressure on myself for some reason. It's like I'm not even competing against everybody else, I'm competing against myself."**

BROADCAST TO THE WORLD

In between competitions, Shaun also found time to make appearances on several television programs and videos. He was featured on an episode of MTV's *Punk'd* and in videos like *White Space* and *Kids Who Rip*.

Shaun even made it to the big screen in December 2005, starring with four other snowboarding **icons** in *First Descent*. The documentary film followed the snowboarders as they rode in Alaska on some of the most dangerous mountains in the world. It also discussed the history of snowboarding from the 1970s to the present day. There was so much footage included in *First Descent* that it took two years to film. The film did fairly well at the box office, and sold well when released on DVD.

MAKING HISTORY AGAIN

The year 2005 had been a great one for Shaun White. He had performed well at both Summer and Winter X Games and won every major snowboarding contest that year. Perhaps the biggest moment was when he stunned the crowd at the U.S. Snowboarding Open by landing four 900s in one halfpipe run—a trick the best snowboarders in the world had been trying to pull off for more than a year.

But as good as 2005 was, 2006 was even better. Shaun started by making history at the Olympic qualifiers. He won every single competition in the five-event Grand Prix series, a feat that had never been accomplished before.

Shaun's victory at the 2006 Winter Olympics in Turin has to be considered one of the biggest, most satisfying wins of his career. He was able to beat out the best athletes in the world and win the gold for the U.S. team. The victory made Shaun an action sports superstar and cemented his status as the best snowboarder in the world. He was only 19 years old at the time.

Shaun also went on to win his fourth consecutive gold medal in the slopestyle contest at the 2006 Winter X Games, and added

Shaun celebrates at the end of a run during the finals of the 2006 Winter Olympics. He later spoke about his feelings as he made his final Olympic halfpipe run. "I never shed tears at events," he said, "but tears were coming down. My family had big, red eyes, too."

CROSS-CURRENTS

To learn about Janna Meyen, the first snowboarder to win four straight X games medals, read "Another Four-Peat Athlete." Go to page 53. ▶▶

another gold in the superpipe contest. This victory made him the first male athlete to win four consecutive gold medals in a single Winter X Games competition. Not surprisingly, Shaun was named Most Outstanding Athlete of Winter X.

Shaun's other major snowboarding wins in 2006 included repeat victories at the U.S. Snowboarding Open and the Vail Sessions. He also won another skateboarding event, the Right Guard Open, a competition on the Dew Tour.

After his Olympic victory, Shaun found that his fame had reached new levels back in the United States. Here, he jokes with Vanessa Minnillo on MTV's Total Request Live (TRL), February 22, 2006. Vanessa is wearing Shaun's Olympic gold medal. Shaun also appeared on many other television shows in the weeks after the Olympics ended.

⇛ RECOGNITION ⇚

Later in 2006, Shaun was recognized for all of his hard work and his successes. He received two ESPN Espy awards in July for Best Male Action Sports Athlete and Best Olympian. Shaun also won the Arby's Action Sports Snowboarder of the Year Award and was named the Rider of the Year by *Transworld Snowboarding*.

At the Guy's Choice Awards hosted by Spike TV, Shaun and skateboarding star Rob Dyrdek were both nominated for the Chairman of the Board award. Shaun ended up with the trophy at the end of the night thanks to all the votes he received from fans.

⇛ GIVING BACK ⇚

In late 2006, Shaun was named the newest global **ambassador** for MOTO RED, a Motorola project. Rock star Bono and advocate Bobby Shriver created the idea of RED products to raise money to fight against AIDS in Africa. Companies like Motorola sell RED products and donate their profits to the cause.

As an ambassador, it was Shaun's responsibility to help spread the word about the project. He was happy to take on the job, calling it an opportunity to make a difference in the world. Motorola was also happy that Shaun was involved in the project. In a press release, Ron Garriques, a Motorola president said:

> **"Shaun White is a sports hero and a role model for many across America. Motorola is proud to have Shaun as an ambassador for MOTO RED. He has genuine belief in the initiative and he wants to make a big difference."**

Shaun has not slowed down since winning Olympic gold. Here, he shows off his trophy after winning the 2007 U.S. Snowboarding Open at Stratton Mountain, Vermont. The win was his second straight in the U.S. Open halfpipe event. Shaun would go on to win the halfpipe competition at the U.S. Snowboarding Open a third time in 2008.

Still Riding High

DURING THE 2005 AND 2006 SEASONS THERE WAS only one snowboarder who consistently made it to the medals podium. That rider was Shaun White. At 20 years old, he was an Olympic gold medalist and the highest-ranked snowboarder in the world. He was also a real contender in several major skateboarding competitions.

Some people might have backed off after winning nearly everything there was to win, but not Shaun. He decided to enter seven major snowboarding events in 2007, as well as a few minor ones. In addition to the contests, Shaun penciled in plans to do more films, as well as snowboard in the backcountry.

⇒ LIFE AS A CELEBRITY ⇐

Shaun's life was more than just snowboarding and skating, however. Eleven months after winning the Olympics, he was still in great demand. He appeared on numerous television shows and was featured in several high-profile magazines. In 2007 Shaun attended a movie premier with former vice president Al Gore, snowboarded with television talk-show host Montel Williams and pop singer Seal, and hung out with celebrity gal pals Lindsay Lohan, Pam Anderson, and Sasha Cohen.

CROSS-CURRENTS

Over the years, Shaun's friends and the media have given him many nicknames. To read about them, see "Shaun's Nicknames." Go to page 54. ▶▶

The newfound fame was a huge boost to Shaun's career. American Express, Hewlett Packard, and other companies wanted him to endorse their products in their commercials. He was also bombarded with requests from video game developers and filmmakers who wanted to work with him on future projects.

Shaun was happy about the attention he was receiving, and appreciated the opportunities that winning the Olympics had provided. Before the 2007 X Games he told a reporter:

> **My schedule has just been slammed, but I couldn't be happier. That's what everybody dreams of, getting that one big break. And I feel like the Olympics did that for me.**

⟫ ANOTHER SUCCESSFUL SEASON ⟪

Shaun had a dream year in 2007. He earned snowboarding's highest honors once again by winning slopestyle and halfpipe competitions at the Burton U.S. Open, the World Superpipe Championship, and the Nippon Open. He also added two more Winter X Games medals to his collection, winning the silver in superpipe and the bronze in slopestyle.

That year, Shaun was named the TTR World Tour Champion and the *Transworld Snowboarding* Rider of the Year. He was also the first competitor to ever win the title of Male Burton Global Open Champion.

⟫ AST SKATE VERT CHAMPION ⟪

There aren't very many snowboarders who can skateboard. Being able to compete in both sports is one of the many things that make Shaun special. But competing wasn't enough for him. He wanted to be the best.

Shaun shows off his skill on rails at a 2007 event held in New York City's Times Square. His high-flying skills and down-to-earth personality have attracted many new fans to the sport of snowboarding. In February thousands of people turned out to watch New York's first professional snowboarding jam, which was held in Central Park.

In other years, Shaun had taken a break between the snowboarding and skateboarding seasons. In 2007, Shaun went straight from snowboarding into skating. He hoped that the extra time would help him win the Summer X games and other skating events. The hard work paid off. Shaun had his best skateboarding season yet.

The season started well when Shaun won first place in the vert competition at the opening stop of the Dew Action Sports Tour. His score of 94.25 was the highest score recorded in the skate vert event on any of the Dew Tour stops. Shaun went on to win the Right Guard Open and the Vans Invitational, the second and third stops on the Dew Tour. His wins earned him enough points in the overall standings to be named the AST Skate Vert Champion.

After failing to land a trick during a skateboarding competition, Shaun bites his helmet in frustration. Overall in 2007 the young skater did not have much to be upset about. He proved that he was among the best skateboarders in the world by winning a gold medal at the 2007 Summer X Games.

≫ CHASING A DREAM ≪

Skating on the Dew Tour kept Shaun's focus sharp for the Summer X Games. He had been disappointed by his performance at the previous year's games and wanted to do better this time around. It was Shaun's dream to have a season in skateboarding like he'd had in snowboarding.

The pressure was on as soon as the skateboard vert competition began. Shaun fell during both his first and second runs, and it looked like his nerves were going to get the best of him. But they didn't. Shaun pulled off an amazing run on his third and final attempt. His score was high enough to earn the Summer X Games gold medal.

The win was an unprecedented accomplishment in action sports. No athlete had ever been able to win a gold medal at both the Summer and Winter X Games. The achievement was proof that Shaun deserved the title of two-sport superstar.

≫ CHARITABLE WORK ≪

But Shaun's focus on his athletic career has not stopped him from giving back to his community. Shaun has been involved in charity work since becoming a professional athlete. In addition to participating in events at Target House, a home away from home for children who are being treated at St. Jude Children's Hospital, he donates and autographs items for organizations like City of Hope, Wings for Life, and Child Safety Network. The items he signs are always given to young children or sold at auctions to raise money for charitable causes.

Shaun is also very active in the Tony Hawk Foundation and has participated in several foundation benefits. One of these is the annual Tony Hawk's Proving Ground Stand Up For Skateparks event. Shaun is a co-chairman of this fundraiser. In October 2007, he put on a vert demonstration at one of the events and entertained the crowd with his daredevil antics. The 2007 Stand Up for Skateparks event attracted celebrities and athletes like Sean "Diddy" Combs, Lance Armstrong, Jamie Lee Curtis, Russell Simmons, and Trent Reznor. It raised more than a million dollars for the Tony Hawk Foundation.

≫ EUROPEAN CHAMP ≪

Shaun remained on top of the world in 2008. He had just turned 21 years old and was the reigning king of both of his sports. At the

Despite his busy schedule, Shaun takes time to help people in need. Here, he participates in Knicks Bowl, a charitable event held each year. Knicks Bowl raises money for the Garden of Dreams Foundation, which provides millions of dollars each year to improve the lives of children in the New York area.

Shaun speaks with an interviewer at the Burton European Open Snowboarding Championship, which was held in Laax, Switzerland. The annual event draws talented snowboarders from all over the world. In 2008 Shaun won the men's slopestyle event, and placed second in the men's halfpipe competition behind fellow American Kevin Pearce.

beginning of the year, Shaun traveled to Switzerland for the Burton European Open, one of the largest snowboarding events in Europe. It is the only snowboarding event on that continent open to all riders.

Although more than 500 riders showed up to compete in the European Open, Shaun was still able to come out on top. He won first place in the slopestyle contest and second place in the halfpipe event. The wins earned him the Burton European Open Overall Champion title as well as a significant amount of prize money and another brand new car.

⋙ X GAMES CONTROVERSY ⋘

Shaun went straight from the European Open to Aspen, Colorado, for the Winter X Games. He had dominated the competition at Winter X for most of his pro career and his past success made him the star of the X Games once again.

Naturally, some of the other snowboarders were jealous about the media attention Shaun received. One of them was rival snowboarder Steve Fisher, who told reporters that other snowboarders deserved attention as well. During the 2008 Winter X Games, Fisher said:

> **The media has turned Shaun into the Tiger Woods of snowboarding. . . . A lot of [the attention] is because he has been such a figure in snowboarding since he was so young. ESPN has really latched onto that story. It's a great story, but there are so many other snowboarders that deserve some time of day.**

However, other snowboarders were quick to defend Shaun, insisting he received the most coverage because he won the most contests. Snowboarder and Olympic medalist J.J. Thomas went as far as to publicly refute Fisher's claims that Shaun didn't deserve the attention, telling a reporter:

> **Most of us have had our share of wins, but Shaun has been able to do it like eight years now. We've all gone through our ups and downs. Shaun has kept it on top the whole time.**

Shaun didn't let the controversy bother him. He won the **bronze medal** in the slopestyle contest. Everyone was impressed with the win because Shaun had accidentally cracked his snowboard just minutes before the event started. He wasn't able to get a replacement and had to ride on a broken board.

The superpipe contest went much better. Shaun got a new board and laid down one of the best runs in Winter X history to win the gold medal. This was the third superpipe gold medal Shaun had won at the Winter X Games. The achievement tied him with skier Tanner Hall for the most gold medals won in the X Games.

⇒ NEW ENDORSEMENTS ⇐

As Shaun was racking up wins at the X Games, his longtime sponsor Target announced the creation of a Shaun White for Target Collection.

From high in the air, Shaun looks to land a trick. At the 2008 Winter X Games, Shaun easily won the men's superpipe event for his seventh career X Games gold. Shaun would go on to win the halfpipe competition at the U.S. Snowboarding Open for the third straight time, and also scored a 2008 Open slope-style victory.

Because of Shaun's famous snowboarding and skateboarding ability, coupled with his great smile and easygoing personality, many companies want him to help sell their products. The young athlete has signed endorsement deals with Burton, Target, and numerous other companies. These agreements provide Shaun with a nice income in addition to his winnings from competitions.

The clothing line, which Shaun helped design, is now sold in Target stores all over the world.

The clothing line was a big deal for Shaun, but the 10-year endorsement contract he signed with Burton Snowboards just two days later was historic. The partnership was the longest deal ever signed by a snowboarder. The endorsement meant that he would continue riding for Burton's Global Team and help the company expand on The White Collection, his signature line of products.

Shaun's income from endorsement deals with Burton, Target, Red Bull, American Express, and other sponsors is estimated to be about $10 million a year. This makes him one of the highest-paid athletes in the world of action sports.

➤ WHAT THE FUTURE HOLDS ◆

Shaun has been skateboarding and having fun on the slopes for more than 14 years. It doesn't seem likely that he will stop anytime soon.

CROSS-CURRENTS

Shaun's main sponsor, Burton, is the world's leading manufacturer of snowboards. To learn more about the company's origins, see "Burton Snowboards." Go to page 55. ▶▶

He has made it clear in interviews that he is interested in representing the United States in the 2010 Winter Olympics, as well as in the 2014 Winter Olympics. Certainly, he is young enough to participate in both games. Shaun will only be 23 when the 2010 Games begin.

There is also a chance that he will participate in the Summer Olympics someday. It has been suggested that skateboarding might make its Olympic debut at the 2012 Summer Games. It is not a sure thing yet, but expectations are high.

In addition to participation in future snowboarding and skateboarding contests, Shaun plans to continue making movies. He is also working with game developer Ubisoft to create an officially licensed Shaun White snowboarding video game for multiple gaming platforms.

Whatever else Shaun decides to do in the future, he will almost certainly continue to be an ambassador for his sports, and a positive role model for young people everywhere.

History of Snowboarding

There is some debate over who created the first snowboard, but most people credit a man named Sherman Poppen. In 1965, Poppen stuck two skis together and tied a rope around them to hold them in place so his daughter could "surf" down a snowy hill in Michigan. Poppen's wife named the homemade contraption a "Snurfer."

It wasn't long before other children were requesting their own Snurfer. Poppen licensed the invention and production of the first snowboards began the very next year. More than 500,000 Snurfers were sold in 1966.

Over the next decade, individuals like Dimitrije Milovich, Jake Burton, and Tom Sims started creating their own Snurfer designs.

Their early attempts would eventually evolve into the boards that snowboarders use today.

As the popularity of the Snurfer grew, snowboarding competitions began to develop. The first World Snurfing Championship was held in 1979. It was followed by the first National Snowboard Race in 1982 and the first World Championship Halfpipe contest in 1983.

By 1985, many people considered snowboarding an "official" winter sport. People from all over the world started to come together regularly to compete in national and international events like the X Games, the U.S. Snowboarding Open, and the Winter Olympics. (Go back to page 5.) ◀◀

Several snowboarding pioneers are pictured in 1983 at the second National Snowboarding Championships (the event would later be called the U.S. Snowboarding Open). Jake Burton, who founded an important snowboard manufacturing company, is on the left. Tom Sims, a champion boarder who some people believe created the first snowboard when he was a middle school student, is on the right.

Making the U.S. Winter Olympic Snowboarding Team

The Winter Olympic Games are held every four years. New competitors are chosen for the U.S. Snowboarding Team every time the games are held.

Snowboarders begin competing for a spot on the team several months before the Olympic Games commence. Team members are usually selected based on their performance in certain snowboarding events and competitions. For example, snowboarders who compete in halfpipe events are chosen for the Olympic team based on their performance in the U.S. Snowboarding Grand Prix, which is the country's premier snowboard series. This selection process allows the U.S. team to choose the strongest competitors from among many talented athletes.

Snowboarders who want to compete in the Olympic Games must also be licensed competitors of the United States Ski and Snowboard Association (USSA) and the International Ski Federation. Other factors that are considered include athletes' physical fitness level, as well as attitude and commitment.

The United States Ski and Snowboard Association develops and publishes the criteria

Snowboarders watch a practice session on the halfpipe before the third Grand Prix snowboarding event of 2006 at Mountain Creek, New Jersey. Snowboarders who want to compete for the American team during the Winter Olympics must prove themselves with top finishes in that season's Grand Prix series of snowboarding events.

for selection to the U.S. Snowboarding Team every four years. To learn more about how athletes make the U.S. Winter Olympic Snowboarding Team, contact the United States Ski and Snowboard Association or visit their website at www.ussa.org. (Go back to page 6.) ◀◀

What Is Tetralogy of Fallot?

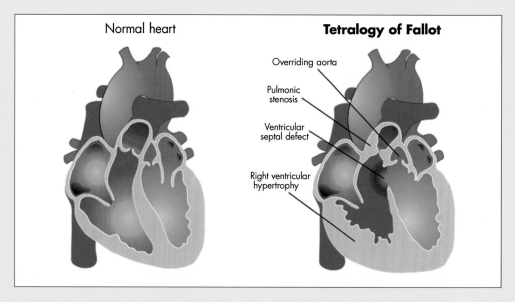

In tetralogy of Fallot, there is a hole (a septal defect) between the heart's ventricles, or pumping chambers. The aorta—the major artery from the heart to the body—lies over the hole. The pulmonary valve, which allows blood to flow through the heart, may be partially blocked. And the right ventricle develops thicker muscle. These problems mean that the infant's blood cannot carry enough oxygen to the body.

Tetralogy of Fallot is a heart condition that is sometimes present in babies. This condition is serious because it affects the way the heart pumps blood and it prevents the bloodstream from having the proper level of oxygen.

The condition can vary from mild to serious. Babies with a mild form of tetralogy of Fallot can go for several years without needing treatment. Other babies need surgery to fix the problem. People who undergo surgery for tetralogy of Fallot can lead normal lives. However, they typically need regular checkups to make sure their repaired hearts are working properly.

Like many other individuals who have been treated for tetralogy of Fallot, Shaun White has been able to put this condition behind him. Shortly before his 2006 Olympic appearance he told a reporter:

> **"It is just something that happened to me in the past and I don't ever think about it. Every two or three years, I need to do a heart test checkup, which is a little weird. Other than that, I've been doing my thing."**

Tetralogy of Fallot is a fairly rare condition. On average, it occurs about three times out of every 10,000 births (.0003 percent). (Go back to page 11.)

History of the X Games

The Summer and Winter X Games are more than just annual sporting events. These competitions are Olympic-like gatherings that allow action sports athletes from all over the world to come together as a community.

The chronology below shows how the X Games evolved from a simple idea in 1993 into two of the world's most exciting action sports events only a few years later:

1993
ESPN conceives an event that will allow extreme athletes to compete in various sports. They call the event the Extreme Games.

1995
The first Extreme Games open on June 24 in Rhode Island. More than 198,000 people show up to watch athletes participate in nine different sports, including biking, sport climbing, bungee jumping, sky surfing, street luge, in-line skating, skateboarding, water sports, and an eco-challenge.

1996
The Extreme Games are renamed the X Games at the beginning of the year and are held in Rhode Island once more. The event receives so much media attention that ESPN decides to hold a winter version of the X Games at Summit Mountain Resort in Big Bear Lake, California.

1997
The first Winter X Games open on January 30. Athletes compete in shovel racing, ice climbing, snowboarding, snow mountain bike racing, and multi-sport crossover events. The Winter X Games are televised in 21 different languages in 198 countries. An estimated 38,000 people show up at Big Bear Lake to watch the athletes compete. The third Summer X Games are held later in the year in San Diego. A record 221,000 people attend the event.

1998
The Winter and Summer X Games both have record attendance in 1998. New sports like snowmobile snocross, freeskiing, and skiboarding debut at Winter X.

1999
The third annual Winter X Games are held in January in Crested Butte, Colorado. The Summer X Games are held in June in San Francisco. Both events draw more attention than ever before.

2000
The Winter X Games are held in February in Mount Snow, Vermont. More than 80,000 people show up to watch the competition. In August, 350 athletes and more than 200,000 spectators arrive in San Francisco for the Summer X Games. By this point, both competitions are firmly established, and their popularity will continue to grow in the coming years.

(Go back to page 15.)

Who Is Tony Hawk?

Tony Hawk is one of the most famous professional skateboarders in the world. He went pro at the age of 14 and was widely considered the world's best skateboarder by the time he was 16. Although Tony has invented more than 80 skateboarding tricks, he is most famous for being the first person to land the 900 on a vert ramp.

In 1999, Tony worked with a company called Activision to create the first Tony Hawk video game. The skateboarding game was an instant success. Nine other Tony Hawk video games have been released since then, and more are planned for the future.

Some of Tony's other businesses include a skateboard company, a clothing line for skaters, and a TV production company. In 2002, he launched an arena tour known as the Boom Boom HuckJam. Some of the world's best skateboarders, BMX riders, and motocross competitors tour with Tony every year.

When he turned 31, Tony retired from competitive skating. However, he still skates for fun and participates in the skateboarding world through the Tony Hawk Foundation. Since it was formed in 2002, the Tony Hawk Foundation has given more than $1.7 million to help build skateparks in low-income communities around the country. (Go back to page 17.)

(Go back to page 17.)

Tony Hawk started skating when he was about nine years old. When he was a teenager Tony was picked for the skating team Bones Brigade. He soon became one of the most famous skaters in America. Today he is retired from competitive skating, but remains involved in several business ventures and charitable projects.

Other Two-Sport Athletes

Two-sport athletes are rare. It takes commitment and an enormous amount of talent to be successful and balance the demands of two sports. This is especially true of professional athletes. Nevertheless, there are athletes besides Shaun White who have tried and succeeded. A few examples include:

Shaun Palmer

Shaun Palmer is a professional snowboarder, skier, mountain biker, and snowmobile driver. He is one of the most highly regarded athletes in action sports. Shaun Palmer is the only competitor to earn gold medals in four different events at the Winter X Games.

Bo Jackson

Vincent Edward "Bo" Jackson played eight seasons of professional baseball and four seasons of professional football in the late 1980s and early 1990s. Bo became one of the most famous multi-sport athletes because of an advertising campaign he did with a sportswear company.

Deion Sanders

Like Bo Jackson, Deion Sanders played both professional football and professional baseball in the 1980s and 1990s. He played 14 seasons in the National Football League (NFL) and nine seasons of Major League Baseball. Deion is the only athlete to play in both the Super Bowl and the World Series.

Althea Gibson

Althea Gibson is known as the "Jackie Robinson of tennis" because she was the first African-American woman to compete on the professional tennis tour. She was very successful, winning 11 major tennis titles during the 1950s. Althea was also the first black woman to play on the Ladies Professional Golf Association (LPGA) tour, appearing in 171 LPGA tournaments between 1963 and 1977.

Babe Didrikson Zaharias

Mildred Ella "Babe" Didrikson Zaharias is often referred to as the greatest all-around female athlete in history. She was accomplished in nearly every sport imaginable, including baseball, basketball, golf, diving, boxing, skating, tennis, track, and volleyball. As a golfer she won 41 LPGA events, including 11 major titles. She also won two gold medals in the track and field competition at the 1932 Olympics.

Jim Thorpe

James Franciscus "Jim" Thorpe is considered to be one of the best all-around athletes of the modern era. In addition to playing professional baseball, basketball, and football between 1913 and 1928, Jim won gold medals in the pentathlon and decathlon events at the 1912 Olympic Games.

(Go back to page 21.)

The Shaun White Album

Shaun has been well known in and out of the world of snowboarding since he was a preteen because of his remarkable talent. But until relatively recently, few people who are not fans of snowboarding or the X Games recognized his name. By 2004, however, growing numbers of people were interested in learning more about the redheaded kid who was being called "the next Tony Hawk."

Shaun gave everyone a sneak peek into his life that year by releasing a movie known as *The Shaun White Album*. The movie follows Shaun's career and includes exclusive footage from family videos, training expeditions, and competitions. There are also interviews with professional skateboarders like Tony Hawk.

The Shaun White Album has a lot of action scenes and includes quite a few funny moments. The movie is not very long—only about 30 minutes—but it is interesting to watch and provides a lot of information about Shaun, as well as about snowboarding and skateboarding.

To see clips from the movie, listen to the soundtrack, or just learn more about *The Shaun White Album*, visit the film's official Web site: www.theshaunwhitealbum.com.

(Go back to page 26.)

Since its release in 2004, The Shaun White Album *has been very popular among snowboarding fans. Over the years Shaun has appeared in several other movies, including* First Descent *(2005),* Kids Who Rip *(2005), and* For Right or Wrong *(2006). Most of his film appearances have come in documentaries that provide a closer look into the world of snowboarding.*

Another Four-Peat Athlete

Shaun White made history by winning four gold medals in a row in the men's slopestyle competition at the X Games—something no other male athlete had ever done. However, he was actually the second person to accomplish the feat of winning four straight X Games medals. The first was Janna Meyen, a female snowboarder.

Janna was born in 1977 and grew up in California. She started snowboarding when she was about 11 years old. In 1991, when Janna was 13, she won the U.S. Snowboarding Open for the first time. Since then, she has racked up so many wins in slopestyle events that she has become known as the "queen of slopestyle." Janna has a fluid style that is very recognizable. She is a tough competitor on the slopes and is considered to be one of the most influential riders in women's snowboarding.

After winning a silver medal at the 2002 X Games slopestyle competition, Janna won gold medals in the same event in 2003, 2004, and 2005. Janna won her fourth gold medal at the 2006 Winter X Games two days before Shaun won his fourth gold.

In 2007, *Snowboarder* magazine selected Janna Meyen as the "most influential female snowboarder of the last 20 years."

(Go back to page 32.)

Janna Meyen has said that the highlight of her snowboarding career was winning her fourth straight Winter X Games gold medal in 2006. She dedicated the win to her grandmother, who was in the hospital at the time. Janna's hopes for a fifth gold medal fell short when she injured her ankle before the 2007 Winter X Games.

Shaun's Nicknames

Over the years Shaun White has had many nicknames. Here are some of the more familiar names he's been known by:

During his career Shaun has had several nicknames. Perhaps the most famous is the "Flying Tomato." The media used this nickname constantly when Shaun won his gold medal at the 2006 Winter Olympics. In fact, the name became so overused that Shaun got tired of hearing it. Today he prefers to be known by his real name.

Future Boy—Shaun was given this nickname when he was still an amateur. The announcers called him this because everyone thought he was the future of snowboarding.

The Egg—This nickname wasn't used for very long. It was a reference to how Shaun's skull looked when he was wearing a helmet.

The Flying Tomato—A couple of Shaun's skater friends gave him this nickname because of his red hair, and it stuck. Shaun used it willingly for a while, even wearing clothing that had the nickname printed on it. He and his friends have since given up the name. However, the media still refers to him as The Flying Tomato every now and then.

Il Pomodoro Volante—Italian for "the Flying Tomato."

Senor Blanco—Spanish for "Mister White."

The Animal—This nickname was given to Shaun after his performance in the 2007 U.S. Snowboarding Open.

Shaun has said that he is ready for a new nickname, but knows he probably shouldn't be the one to come up with it. In an interview with *Rolling Stone*, he joked, "I'd just come up with something bad, like 'Incredibly Handsome Man.'"

(Go back to page 36.)

Burton Snowboards

Burton Snowboards creates and manufactures snowboarding equipment. Jake Burton Carpenter, one of the world's first snowboarders, founded the company. Jake began snowboarding during the 1960s. In 1977, he founded Burton Snowboards.

The company's sales were slow at first. Snowboarding was just emerging as a sport, and it often wasn't permitted at ski resorts. Jake and other pioneers of the sport had to work hard to get the rules changed. Their efforts finally began to pay off during the early 1980s. National snowboarding championships were organized and resorts began to allow snowboarders on the slopes. Today, Burton is the world's leading manufacturer of snowboards and snowboarding accessories.

Burton Snowboards has supported Shaun White for a long time. The company gave him his first properly sized snowboard, as well as his first sponsorship. As Shaun has become one of the biggest names in action sports, he has returned the company's loyalty. He still rides for the Burton team and has never used a board that wasn't made by Burton.

Shaun's older brother, Jesse, is also committed to Burton Snowboards. Jesse White has worked for the snowboard company for many years, managing riders and helping Shaun design new snowboards and equipment. (Go back to page 45.) ◀◀

Members of a Belgian team pose with their Burton snowboards. The company's Web site describes Burton as "a rider driven company solely dedicated to creating the best snowboarding equipment on the planet." Snowboarder Jake Burton founded the company in 1977, opening a small facility in Vermont to build and repair snowboards. Today, Burton Snowboards has stores all over the world.

1986 Shaun Roger White is born on September 3 in Carlsbad, California.

1992 Six-year-old Shaun learns how to snowboard.

1993 Shaun enters and wins his first official amateur snowboarding competition.

2000 At the age of 13, Shaun gives up amateur snowboarding competitions for professional competitions and accepts an endorsement deal from Burton.

2001 Shaun finishes in the top ten in two different events at the Winter X Games.

2002 After winning his first two Winter X Games medals, Shaun joins Tony Hawk's Gigantic Skate Park Tour.

2003 Shaun becomes the youngest U.S. Open Slopestyle champion.

2004 After winning a gold medal at the Winter X Games and taking first in several other snowboarding competitions, including the Honda Session Rail Jam and the Innsbruck Air and Style, Shaun releases an acclaimed snowboarding movie titled *The Shaun White Album*.

2005 Shaun qualifies for the U.S. Winter Olympic team and becomes the first athlete to win a medal at both the Summer and the Winter X Games.

2006 Shaun has a dream year in snowboarding, winning every competition he enters, including the U.S. Olympics Halfpipe, the Winter X Games Superpipe and Slopestyle, the U.S. Open Halfpipe and Slopestyle, and the Honda Session Slopestyle.

2007 Shaun becomes the first person to ever to win a gold medal at both the Summer X Games and the Winter X Games, and the first person ever to sweep the snowboard events in the Grand Prix halfpipe season.

2008 Shaun wins gold in the Winter X superpipe competition and bronze in the Winter X slopestyle competition; Shaun is also named the Burton European Open Overall Champ.

2009 Shaun wins his second gold medal in the Winter X superpipe competition and his first gold medal in the Winter X slopestyle competition.

In April, Shaun chips a bone in his ankle and begins his recuperation.

2010 Shaun wins the gold medal in the halfpipe competition at the 2010 Winter Olympics in Vancouver.

Winter X Games Medals

2002 Superpipe silver, Slopestyle silver
2003 Superpipe gold, Slopestyle gold
2004 Slopestyle gold
2005 Slopestyle gold
2006 Superpipe gold, Slopestyle gold
2007 Superpipe silver, Slopestyle bronze
2008 Superpipe gold, Slopestyle bronze
2009 Superpipe gold, Slopestyle gold

Summer X Games Medals

2005 Vert competition silver
2007 Vert competition gold

Global X Games Medals

2003 Superpipe gold

Selected Awards

2003 ESPN ESPY Award for Best Action Sports Athlete
Outstanding Athlete of the Winter X Games

2004 *Sports Business Journal*'s Most Influential People in Action Sports
Sports Illustrated for Kids' Best on Board

2005 *Ad Age* Top 10 Prospect

2006 U.S. Olympic Spirit Award
Outstanding Athlete of the Winter X Games
ESPN ESPY Award for Best Male Action Sports Star and Best U.S. Olympian
Arby's Action Sports Snowboarder of the Year Award
Transworld Snowboarding Rider of the Year

2007 *Snowboarder Magazine* Top Ten Rider of the Year
Spike TV Guy's Choice Awards Chairman of the Board
Transworld Snowboarding Rider of the Year

2008 Laureus World Action Sportsperson of the Year Award

2010 Olympic Gold, halfpipe competition

Books

Doeden, Matt. *Shaun White*. Minneapolis: Lerner, 2006.

Fitzpatrick, Jim. *Shaun White*. Mankato, Minn.: The Child's World, 2008.

Lebenthal, Claudia, and Daniel Stark. *Stoked: The Evolution of Action Sports*. New York: Empire Editions, 2006.

Maxwell, E. J. *Xtreme Sports: Cutting Edge*. New York: Scholastic, 2003.

Reed, Rob. *The Way of the Snowboarder*. New York: HNA Books, 2005.

Web Sites

http://www.shaunwhite.com

Shaun White's official Web site includes a blog, photos, and snowboarding videos, as well as news about Shaun's career.

http://www.theshaunwhitealbum.com

The official Web site of *The Shaun White Album* features clips and information about the movie and soundtrack.

http://www.usolympicteam.com

The official Web site of the U.S. Olympic Team offers a bio for Shaun White, as well as photos, notes, and quotes.

http://www.snowboardermag.com/shaunwhite/

The Web site for *Snowboarder Magazine* has an entire page devoted to Shaun White. The page includes interviews with Shaun, photo galleries, exclusive videos, and much more.

http://expn.com

The official Web site for the X Games includes plenty of information about Shaun's snowboarding and skateboarding prowess.

---

action sport—a term for sports that involve a certain level of danger, often involving speed, height, a high level of physical exertion, spectacular stunts, and weather- or terrain-related variables that affect the outcome.

ambassador—someone who is regarded as a representative of an organization, or program.

atrophy—the shrinking in size of muscles, often caused by lack of use due to injury.

big air—an exceptionally high jump.

bronze medal—an award given to the third-place finisher in a competition.

documentary—a film that prevents facts or information about real people or events, rather than telling a fictional story.

endorse—to give public support or approval of a product, usually in an advertisement to promote that product.

gold medal—an award given to an individual or team who wins a competition.

halfpipe—a u-shaped ramp with high sides. Halfpipes can be found in skateboarding, snowboarding, BMX riding, and in-line skating.

icon—a person who is widely recognized and admired.

McTwist—a popular skateboarding or snowboarding trick that involves a front flip combined with a 540° rotation.

shredding—a slang expression used to refer to a snowboard ride that is particularly intense, aggressive, or skillful.

silver medal—an award given to second-place finisher in a competition.

slopestyle—a freestyle snowboarding event that requires riders to perform tricks while riding a downhill course over a variety of different jumps.

sponsor—in sports, a corporation or organization that pays some or all of an athlete's training and competition expenses. In return, the athlete typically represents the sponsor in various events and contests.

superpipe—a very large halfpipe.

switch—riding a skateboard or snowboard backwards.

unprecedented—something that has never happened before.

vert competition—a skateboarding competition that requires riders to perform tricks on a vertical ramp.

page 4 "I'm a little overwhelmed . . ." Eddie Pells, "Flying Tomato Golden in Torino," Associated Press (February 12, 2006). www.usolympicteam.com/11471_44321.htm.

page 6 "Going into a 1080 . . ." Yi-Wyn Yen, "Hot Tomato: Shaun White's Otherworld Talents and Trademark Red Hair Have Made Him the Boarder to Watch in the Olympic Halfpipe." *Sports Illustrated* 104, no. 2 (January 16, 2006), p. 65.

page 7 "I'm just dropping in . . ." Mark Zeigler, "Taking Flight: Board-Sports Icon Shaun White, 19, Leads U.S. to 1-2 Finish in Halfpipe." *San Diego Union Tribune* (February 13, 2006), p. C1.

page 9 "I didn't know if . . ." U.S. Snowboarding, "*White Wins Gold, Kass Silver in Halfpipe*," (press release). Available at www.ussnowboarding.com/public/news.php?&dId=7&aId=1949.

page 9 "I woke up and . . ." Justin Tejada, "White Gold Snowboarder: Shaun White Soared to a Gold Medal at the Winter Olympics" *Sports Illustrated for Kids* 18, no. 4 (April 2006), p. 15.

page 9 "I think it's fun . . ." Justin Tejada, "White Hot: Shaun White Is Enjoying Life as an Action Sports Superstar." *Sports Illustrated for Kids* 18, no. 8 (August 2006), p. 20.

page 12 "He taught me . . ." Mary Catherine O'Connor, "Mountainzone.com Interview with Shaun White." Available at http://classic.mountainzone.com/snowboarding/2000/interviews/white/.

page 12 "We almost didn't take . . ." O'Connor, "Mountainzone.com Interview with Shaun White."

page 15 "I wanted to be recognized . . ." "Shaun White: the 15-Year-Old Snowboarding Phenom Is Stoked to Drop into the Olympic Halfpipe." *Sports Illustrated for Kids* 14, no. 2 (February 2002), p. 48.

page 17 "Even five years ago . . ." Gavin Edwards, "*Shaun White: Attack of the Flying Tomato.*" *Rolling Stone* 995 (March 9, 2006), p. 43.

page 18 "I've always wanted to . . ." Ursula Liang, "Snowboard Slopestyle Men's Finals." Available at http://expn.go.com/xgames/wxg/vii/s/030202_snbstylem.html.

page 21 "It was my first pro . . ." Chris Coyle, "The Shaun White Interview." Available at www.transworldsnowboarding.com/snow/features/article/0,26719,516123,00.html.

page 23 "Most of my money . . ." Coyle, "The Shaun White Interview."

page 26 "I had such a . . ." Justin Tejada, "24 Hours with Shaun White." *Sports Illustrated for Kids* 17, no. 3 (March 1, 2005), p. T6.

page 27 "I was so scared . . ." Pat Bridges, "The Next Shaun White." Available at www.snowboarding.com/magazine/features/shaun-white.

page 30 "I put tons of . . ." Bridges, "The Next Shaun White."

page 31   "I never shed tears . . ." Sal Ruibal, "Early Jitters Add Drama to White's Golden Run," USA Today (February 13, 2006), p. E7.

page 33   "Shaun White is a . . ." Motorola, "From Gold Medalist to MOTO Red." (press release). Available at http://www.webwire.com/ViewPressRel.asp?aId=24277.

page 36   "My schedule has just . . ." Vicki Michaelis, "White's Afterglow Still Golden." Available at www.usatoday.com/sports/olympics/winter/2007-01-23-white-celebrity_x.htm.

page 42   "The media has turned . . ." Brian Gomez, "Shaun White's Fame Upsets Some of His Winter X Games Competitors." Colorado Springs Gazette (January 27, 2008), p. C1.

page 42   "Most of us have . . ." Gomez, "Shaun White's Fame Upsets Some of His Winter X Games Competitors," p. C1.

page 48   "It is just something . . ." Bridges, "The Next Shaun White."

page 55   "a rider driven company . . ." Burton Snowboards Web site, http://www.burton.com/Company/CompanyHome.aspx.

Numbers in ***bold italics*** refer to captions.

Karen Schweitzer has written numerous articles for magazines and newspapers, including the *Erickson Tribune* and *Learning Through History*, and for Web sites like About.com. She is also the author of several books, including *The Shih Tzu* (Eldorado Ink, 2009) and a biography of Sheryl Swoopes in Mason Crest's MODERN ROLE MODELS series. Karen lives in Michigan with her husband. You can learn more about her at *www.karenschweitzer.com*.

PICTURE CREDITS

page

1: Getty Images
4: Joe Klamar/AFP/Getty Images
7: Joe Klamar/AFP/Getty Images
8: Elsa/Getty Images
10: Burton/PRMS
13: T&T/IOA Photos
14: Burton/PRMS
16: Bo Bridges/SPCS
19: Bo Bridges/SPCS
22: Target/NMI
24: Jeff Curtes/SPCS
27: Cinemaseoane/PRMS
29: Dew Action Sports Tour/SPCS
31: Agence Zoom/Getty Images
32: Scott Gries/Getty Images

34: Burton/PRMS
37: CIC Photos
38: Ken Blaze/Lat34/SPCS
40: NBAE/Getty Images
41: Chris/Burton/PRMS
43: Jess Mooney/SPCS
44: Ben Liebenberg/WireImage
46: Hubert Schriebl/Burton/PRMS
47: Lauren Traub/SPCS
48: MedGraphic
50: Silverdocs/NMI
52: Dean "Blotto" Gray/SPCS
53: etinies/PRMS
54: Dew Action Sports Tour/SPCS
55: Burton/PRMS

Front cover: Doug Pensinger/AFP/Getty Imags